The Road t

Written by Lesa Cline-Ransome
Illustrated by
John Charles, Sylvia Szakall and Janos Orban

Published by Pearson Education Limited,
80 Strand, London, WC2R 0RL.

www.pearsonschools.co.uk

Text © Pearson Education Limited 2016

Original illustrations © Pearson Education Limited
Illustrated by John Charles, Sylvia Szakall and Janos Orban

First published in the USA by Pearson Education Inc, 2016
First published in the UK by Pearson Education Ltd, 2017

21 20 19 18 17
10 9 8 7 6 5 4 3 2 1

British Library Cataloguing in Publication Data
A catalogue record for this book is available from the British Library

ISBN 978 0 435 18652 4

Copyright notice
All rights reserved. No part of this publication may be reproduced
in any form or by any means (including photocopying or storing it
in any medium by electronic means and whether or not transiently
or incidentally to some other use of this publication) without the
written permission of the copyright owner, except in accordance
with the provisions of the Copyright, Designs and Patents Act 1988
or under the terms of a licence issued by the Copyright Licensing
Agency, Barnards Inn, 86 Fetter Lane, London EC4A 1EN
(www.cla.co.uk). Applications for the copyright owner's written
permission should be addressed to the publisher.

Printed in China by Golden Cup

Contents

Prologue

The Underground Railroad began in the 1780s and continued until the start of the American Civil War in 1861. Thousands of abolitionists (those who worked to abolish slavery, including Quakers, free blacks, slaves and many others) took tremendous risks to ensure safe passage for runaways fleeing slavery.

Though the events of this story are fictional, the methods of escape are based on actual, historical accounts of those who fled from slavery on the Underground Railroad. The exact number of slaves who escaped using the Underground Railroad is unknown, but historians estimate the number to be nearly 100,000. An elaborate system of signals and codes, including references to the "drinking gourd" as a symbol of the Big Dipper constellation that points to the North Star, helped to keep the Underground Railroad's operations secret.

When the Fugitive Slave Act was passed in 1850, escaped slaves who had made it to freedom in the North were in fear of being captured and returned to slavery in the South. The only way to truly be safe from their slave masters was to run further north into "Freedom's Land", or Canada, which had abolished slavery in 1833. By 1852, an estimated 25,000 fugitives were living in Canada.

Harriet Tubman, often called "Moses" because she led so many of her people to freedom, was one of the most celebrated conductors of the Underground Railroad. At the age of 28, she escaped alone by walking to Pennsylvania. She completed at least fifteen trips back to her native Maryland, rescuing nearly 300 slaves, including many of her family members. She bought a home in Auburn, New York, not far from the border of Canada.

Chapter 1

Ever since Mama came back to the quarters, she'd been fretting. There was talk in the fields and folks were saying the master had money troubles. They said selling slaves was the only way he could pay his debts. Last month the master had sold Uncle Jacob and his woman Mary. They were old and didn't fetch a good price on the auction block, but this time he was selling the younger ones. Mama knew that meant the master was planning to sell Lula's two boys, Miss Bessie's new baby and me.

I told Mama not to worry. "It's just talk is all, Mama," I said, hoping she didn't see my hand shaking while I stirred the supper, but she didn't stop fretting that night or the next nights either.

Papa had been gone for two winters now. Before he left, he and Mama sat in the cabin by the lantern most nights, talking soft so I couldn't hear. On my pallet, I kept my eyes closed but my ears were open, listening.

"We follow this road here along the creek." Papa scratched with a stick on the dirt floor of our cabin for Mama. "Someone will be waiting there."

Papa talked to folks, and slaves who travelled, and runaways too. He talked real quietly about how to run, and which way north is best.

Then one day, when Mama got back from the field, Papa was gone. The master had sold him south, and he'd taken him from the yard where he worked shoeing horses. We never got a chance to say goodbye. Me and Mama cried so hard, I thought we'd never stop. After that, there was no more talk about running.

But now, with folks talking about the auction block, Mama said they'd sell me and she'd never see me again.

"We're all the family each other have, Emma," Mama said, looking deep into my eyes.

She took my hand and we knelt on the cabin floor, praying long and hard into the night for mercy and deliverance. When we turned the lantern down and settled on our pallets, Mama slept soundly for the first night all week.

When she woke in the morning, Mama told me she had a dream about a drinking gourd, a quilt on a fence and a river as wide as a road. She said that it was a sign, showing her the way north, to freedom.

"We gotta run," she told me. "We leave tonight."

Never in my life had a day felt so long. Each hour felt like two and my mouth was dry just thinking about running. Me and Mama knew that most who ran didn't make it. The runaways they caught came back and were punished hard. No one who was caught ever ran again.

When Mama came back from turning the fields, she put aside some ash cake and a bit of salted meat. We each put on an extra shift, and Mama wrapped my feet with cloth. The chill hit us as soon as we opened the door to the night, but chances were better if we travelled in the cold, when the river turned to ice and was hard enough to cross on foot.

That night, we left with our food tied tight in a scarf, the clothes on our backs and only the North Star to guide us.

Chapter 2

I followed behind Mama, holding onto the back of her shawl so I wouldn't stumble. Real quiet, we passed rows of cabins and then ducked quickly into the woods nearby. Mama moved so fast I could barely keep up, and as we ran, I kept looking behind, hoping no one was following. Up above, the owls called out, and beneath our feet branches and twigs cracked and snapped with each step. We stopped now and again to catch our breath and then continued.

The cloths on my feet didn't hold, so then I had to run barefoot. I didn't wear shoes on the plantation and my feet were rough and hard, but I could still feel every rock on the freezing cold ground. We ran for so long and so far, I was sure we were in the North by now, but Mama said we still had days and days to go. I didn't tell Mama, but I wasn't sure I could take another step. I knew Mama was tired too, but thinking about what was behind us kept her going. We reached a spot where the ground was soft and I knew we were close to water. Croaking frogs and slithering sounds were all around us, and tree branches hung low as we pushed moss out of the way and walked through to the river's edge.

The ice on the river was slick and smooth and it burned my bare feet with its cold. We walked as fast as we could without slipping, but the wind was so strong, I had to hold on to Mama to keep from being blown away. Halfway across we heard ice crack beneath us and we backed up till we stood on the hard ice again.

Mama said, "You are so light, Emma – you go on across first and I'll follow behind. Better we go one at a time."

I started out, stepping as lightly as I could until I got to the solid part. But when Mama

crossed, all I could hear was the cracking until
she stopped, frozen and scared.

"Walk faster, Mama!" I yelled from where I
stood. But just as Mama went to take a step,
the ice broke. She jumped off the broken
piece onto another piece, and then another.
From what I could see, she hopped from one
foot to the next, trying to keep from slipping
into the water. I stopped breathing, waiting,
hoping she'd make it across 'cause if she
stopped, she'd sink into the river for sure.
She was closer now, and I stepped forward,
reaching out my hand to Mama. Only when
I felt her hand in mine did I start breathing
again, and I hung onto her, crying.

"It's all right, Emma," she hugged back. "I'm just fine." I looked at her wet skirts where she'd dipped below the ice, and I knew we had to hurry to land.

On the other side I listened to the night sounds all around us, scared of the dark for the first time.

Our fingers were stiff with cold but we gathered up some sticks and leaves – whatever we could find to  cover us from the slave catchers before the sun came up. They patrolled the woods and roads all day and night hoping to find someone out, away from the plantation, and there was no telling where they'd be and when. Mama pointed to a tree that was broken in half, and we placed the sticks against it and covered it with leaves. Shivering, we squeezed in and lay

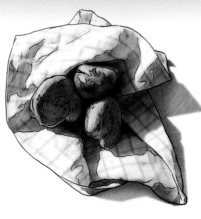

on the hard ground, covering ourselves with more leaves. We ate some of the ash cake and held each other to stay warm. I tried not to think of my pallet back in our cabin and the warmth of a fire.

Mama's eyes were red and puffy. "You sleep, Mama," I said, the taste of dirt in my mouth. "I'll listen out."

"You sure, Emma?" she asked, her voice heavy with sleep.

I told her I'd wake her as soon as I got sleepy, and no sooner had I said it than Mama curled up, trying to stay warm. While Mama's breath got heavier, I sat up and listened. To stay awake, I thought of the master, the slave catchers and their dogs. Then I thought of Papa and wondered if he'd ever made it to freedom like my friend Hetty. When Hetty left last winter with her ma, I prayed for her safety. Every day I watched for her, missing her but hoping they didn't catch her and bring her back. I closed my eyes, pretending we were all together – me, Mama, Papa and Hetty, up north, free from the master. Before I knew it, sleep was on me.

Chapter 3

I woke to the sound of dogs.

"Mama, wake up!" I shook her and she jumped. She looked around, scared. We had no time to run so Mama quickly covered us with leaves, and then we curled up tight, with our knees to our chests, trying to make ourselves small. Best I could tell, the dogs were on the other side of the river.

We curled closer, hoping the master and his catchers wouldn't come our way.

The sun was bright above us and without the night sounds the crunching leaves and cracking twigs sounded louder. I wondered how long I had slept, wondered how long the dogs had been barking, and wondered if the dogs could still track us even though we'd crossed the icy river.

"I'm sorry, Mama," I whispered, letting the tears run down my cheeks. "I tried to stay awake, but . . . "

Mama just pulled me to her. The sound of men's voices and barking dogs got closer.

I knew all about the catchers. How they searched for runaways and returned them to plantations for money. I held my breath and lay as still as a possum, waiting. We waited until I didn't think I could lie still any longer and then, bit by bit, the sound of men talking and dogs sniffing got softer and further away. I opened my mouth to say something, but Mama covered it with her hand. We waited a little longer until we heard nothing but the screech of birds above us.

Finally, Mama said, "During the day, we gotta stay outta sight, but tonight, when it's dark, we make our way to the creek."

My stomach grumbled and Mama handed me the last of the food. I shook my head no, but Mama pushed it into my hand. "Eat, Emma. You're gonna need it," she said. I shoved every last bit in my mouth, hoping to stop the pain in my empty stomach. As soon as we got settled, I heard thunder.

Chapter 4

The rain poured in buckets from the sky and soaked through every inch of us.

"Thank you, thank you," Mama cried, her arms raised towards the sky.

"For the rain?" I asked, shivering.

"For covering our tracks and our scent. Can't no dogs find us now," she said.

We started out when the sun set, but with the clouds covering the sky, I couldn't find the North Star. We ran, following 'longside the road, slipping through mud and wet leaves. Every time we stopped to catch our breath, Mama rubbed her hands along the trunk of a tree.

"Mama, what are you doing?" I asked, panting.

"Making sure we're headed north. The moss grows on the north side of these here trunks. When we don't have the North Star, we're gonna use these trees to lead us."

I reached out and felt the spongy moss on the trunk.

"That way?" I pointed up ahead. Mama nodded and we took off running again. The rain finally slowed to a stop but our dresses were wet and heavy as rocks.

Mama stopped. "You hear that?" I listened close and just when I was about to shake my head no, I heard it. A soft rippling sound. "Water?" I whispered. Mama nodded and we hurried our steps. This was the creek we needed to follow.

I pretended I didn't feel scared in my chest. After a while, we smelled fire from a chimney, and high on a hill, we saw a house with a lantern in the window. We held hands as we crossed the creek, slipping on rocks. Finally, we made it to the other side. We climbed the hill towards the house, grabbing hold of tree roots and clumps of dirt. Mama reached the top first and pulled me up. The house sat in front of us, bigger up close. We hid behind a group of trees and waited.

"What are we waiting for, Mama?" I whispered in her ear. Mama didn't answer.

More time passed and an old white woman came out. She carried a quilt in one arm and a quilt beater in the other and when she reached the fence, she hung the quilt over, beat it a few times, and walked back to the house.

"It's safe," Mama said and started towards the house as I hurried behind.

We went around back and knocked soft three times. Just as Mama was about to knock again, the door opened.

"Welcome," the old woman said, and pulled us inside.

Chapter 5

The house was warm. The old woman helped us undress and hung our clothes up to dry. After days of eating ash cake, her hot, salty stew warmed my insides.

Her kindly face looked worried as she checked my feet for cuts, wrapping a soft bandage where a rock had cut deep. She said she was a Quaker. I'd never heard of a Quaker before, but I guessed they must be mighty kind folks to help people run from slavery.

"We believe it is wrong for one person to enslave another," she explained.

While we ate, she told us her house was a station on the Underground Railroad. Only this railroad had no trains and no tracks. Its conductors were people who thought slavery was wrong and wanted to help runaways. She didn't know how many she'd helped get to the North. "Not enough," she'd said sadly.

Suddenly we heard horses outside.

"Hurry," the old woman whispered. She moved the table and rug to the side and pulled on a latch on the floor. "Go quickly," she said, handing us our clothes. We made our way down steps into a small space beneath the floorboards. The space was so small we could hardly stand and as soon as we were down, she shut the door and pulled the rug and table on top, enclosing us in darkness.

A group of men, talking loudly, banged on the door. "Open up!" deep voices yelled.

"Give an old woman a chance to gather herself," she said, slowly shuffling towards the door.

We heard voices above us, angry and mean. I heard glass break and a chair knocked over.

"But I've not seen any runaways," the woman said. More voices and then a door slammed. We waited in the dark, staring up at the door until the rug and table moved away and light crept through the slats.

"It's not safe," the woman said to Mama, her face as sad as my heart. "Stay the night and tomorrow you'll move to another station."

Again, me and Mama slept curled up together on a blanket, but our bellies were full and we were warm. In my sleep, I dreamed of barking dogs and the master.

We woke when the morning light crept through the open door.

"Come quickly," the woman said. "A friend outside will take you further."

She handed me boots that were worn but strong and sturdy.

"You'll be needing these for the cold up north," she smiled. "Peace be with you both."

We hurried to the waiting wagon. The driver nodded to the pile of potatoes in the back. He moved them aside and we lay flat. He covered us with a scratchy burlap cloth and piled the potatoes on top. Then I heard the snap of the reins, and we were off.

Chapter 6

The road was bumpy. My head banged against
the side of the wagon, and the burlap tickled
my nose. It felt like the wagon hit every stone
and rut as we travelled along. The wagon
slowed and came to a stop. I turned my head
to Mama, and the potatoes tumbled above.

The mules whinnied next to the wagon, and then we heard voices. "Whatcha got back there?" a man asked the driver.

"Just heading to market is all," the driver replied.

"You seen any runaways 'long this road?" the man asked. "A woman and her girl 'bout this high?"

"No sir, can't say I have."

"Mind if I have a look at what you're taking to market?" the man asked.

"Yessir . . . I mean no, sir," the driver stuttered.

Though it was cold, my back was wet with sweat. I heard Mama breathe in deep and I felt potatoes move to the side.

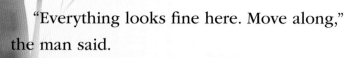

"Everything looks fine here. Move along," the man said.

"Yessir. Good day, sir," the driver replied.

The wagon started up again, moving faster now.

When we got down the road a bit, I sneezed.

Chapter 7

The wind whipped above us as we rode into the night. Every now and again we'd pass another wagon on the road, but mostly we were all alone. The steady clop of the mules' hooves and the creak of the wagon were the only sounds we heard.

"Where we heading, Mama?" I whispered.

"Don't know for sure, but we got to be close now," she answered.

I had just drifted off to sleep again when I felt the wagon stop and heard the driver's boots crunching the snow as he made his way to us. He moved the potatoes, then the cloth, and offered his hand.

"This is as far as I go," he said.

We climbed out, stiff and sore. When my eyes adjusted I saw a stretch of land. The stars and moon were bright above us. With so few trees for cover, I wondered how we'd hide.

"Go through the field till you come to a barn. If the lantern is lit, go on inside. Someone will be waiting and they'll know what to do from there."

We thanked him. I wished I had something to give him for his kindness and without waiting, I stepped forward and hugged him. He smiled then, and climbed onto the wagon.

"Y'all be careful now. Catchers ride along these roads, so make your way quick." He snapped the reins and was gone.

Mama grabbed my hand and we ran across the field. It seemed like my legs couldn't move as fast after lying still for so long, but finally we saw a big barn behind a white house.

"Is that it?" I asked Mama.

"Reckon so. I see a lantern," she said.

The wide doors creaked as we opened
them. Once we were inside, we closed the
doors and headed up to the hayloft. Mice
scattered everywhere, but this time I stayed
quiet and followed Mama up the ladder. We
pulled two bales of hay in front of us and lay
down to wait.

"What if no one comes?" I whispered in the
dark. "What if this is the wrong barn?"

"Emma, we got no choice but to trust.
We give it some time and then we got to
keep going, same as we have been," Mama
whispered back.

We heard steps outside and then a voice,
singing.

"Swing low, sweet chariot
Coming for to carry me home,
Swing low, sweet chariot
Coming for to carry me home . . ."

The barn doors creaked open and a small person, dressed in a heavy coat and hat, walked towards the ladder of the hayloft. Mama looked down.

"I'm a friend," a woman's voice said. "My name is Harriet, and you need to come with me now."

Chapter 8

Back on the plantation, when Papa was still with us, he told Mama about a woman called Harriet Tubman who'd escaped and came back south again and again, bringing folks north to freedom. Papa said she never lost a passenger. I hoped Mama and I would be safe with her.

Miss Harriet had friends everywhere we went, but we still had to be careful. She showed us how to watch for a light in a window or a flag blowing in the wind to know if we were safe. We slept in barns and hid away in attics. Sometimes Miss Harriet would change clothes and look like a man. Sometimes she'd use a cane and walk hunched over like an old woman. It was no wonder she couldn't be caught by bounty hunters – she was always one step ahead. In one home where we hid, someone said there was a $40,000 reward for capturing her. I couldn't count much, but I knew that was a whole heap of money.

We crossed rivers and walked till my feet were covered in blisters, but, tired as we were, Harriet never let us stop.

"How much longer?" I'd ask when I got tired.

Harriet answered by walking faster.

One night, with a light snow falling
all around us, we crossed into the North.
"Philadelphia," Harriet called it. Philadelphia
was filled with people and houses all close
together. A lot of the people were free
Negroes, dressed fine. Looked like freedom
had a way of making them walk a little bit
taller. Mama looked different too – proud that
she'd made it to freedom and happy to have
me beside her, safe from the auction block.

Just when we got settled in with a friend of Harriet's, she sat us down.

"Your journey's not over yet," she told us. "Your master is still looking and he posted a reward for you both," she said. "Even though you're in the North, the law says your master still has claims on you, so the only way you can really be safe is if you go on, into Canada."

Mama nodded, like she already knew.

"Are you coming with us?" I asked.

Harriet shook her head no and told us she was heading back south. There were more people who needed her help. Mama and I would be alone again.

A carriage brought us through town and to the train depot. A real train this time on real tracks that would take us all the way to New York. Harriet had friends on this train who could help us once we reached Buffalo, and from there we would be taken to cross the river into Canada.

We climbed aboard the last car, and Harriet handed us blankets and food. Mama turned to say something to Harriet, but before we knew it, she was gone.

Chapter 9

Hidden beneath blankets and surrounded by sacks, we sat on the hard floor of the train car. We heard the long toot of the horn as it pulled out of the station. I'd never moved so fast, and my stomach turned and twisted with the train. Mama offered me food, but for the first time since we ran, I couldn't eat. I was tired and sore. I looked over at Mama. Her head rested on her knees and her boots were nearly worn clean through. Her dress, dirty and torn, hung on her loose like a sack. She looked up to see me staring and smiled.

"You were real strong, Emma," she said. "Your papa would have been proud."

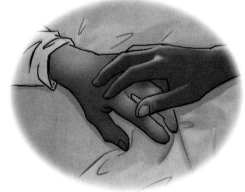

I smiled back. "You too, Mama," I said.

She reached for my hand. "Almost there," she whispered.

Every once in a while, me and Mama would peek through the crack in the car, hoping to see something. There was never anything to see but trees and more land. Hard to tell Buffalo from where we'd come.

Another day dawned and the train slowed to a stop. We waited. Was this our stop? Mama got up to look, and the door to the train car opened. Outside a man waited. His skin was brown like mine and his hair was as white as the moon. He led us to his carriage and helped us up.

The day was still and grey and all the trees were bare.

"I'll take you up to Lewiston, to the Niagara crossing," he said. "Make it across and you are in free territory. You need to find a house with four pillars. From there you'll row 'cross the river."

He helped us down and we gathered our blankets and the last of our food. He turned to his carriage and rode away, humming a song.

"O Canaan, sweet Canaan,
I am bound for the land of Canaan."

When we saw the house with four pillars in front of us, I squeezed Mama's hand. I couldn't believe freedom was across the water. I didn't know what our new life in Canada would be, but I knew as I boarded that little rowing boat that whatever it was, I was safe now from the auction block and we were together. The sun was setting and up above us the North Star was shining bright. We rowed towards Canada and into freedom.